It was rare for Eldita to be impolite
so Granny Olla gave her a good-hearted smile
and said, "Maybe the heat made me forget."

Eldita scowled and stomped up the stairs.

3

"Mum, I'm hungry!" said Eldita.

Her mother replied, "We only have
some leftover onion soup.
Would you like that?"

"Don't you have any fruit or eggs?"
said Eldita.

Food was scarce in most households in Havana, Cuba.
People couldn't get fuel for their cars and vans
so crops and produce wasn't carried to town
and the grocery shops had bare shelves.

ıto

y Christopher Corr
dited by Joy Cowley

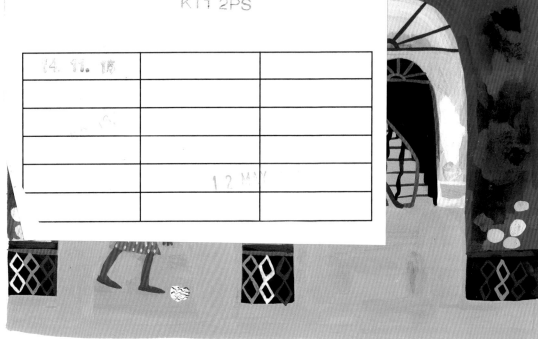

When Eldita came home from her ballet lesson,
she wasn't smiling like usual.
Granny Olla said, "Isn't it hot today?"
Eldita replied, "Didn't you have a shower?"

The Soviet Union was Cuba's supporter and ally. When the Soviet Union disbanded in the early 1990s, the people of Cuba were at risk of starvation. International trade reduced by half, and 80 per cent of factories closed due to lack of oil. Crops rotted in the fields because they could not be delivered, so they weren't harvested.

Eldita's mother shrugged and hung up the washing.
Eldita shouted, "Tina got the main role today!"

Her mum replied, "Tina deserves the main role.
You know that she's a very good dancer."

It was true, and Eldita knew it, but she said,
"She can dance like that because she eats so well.
Her dad drives a taxi and he makes lots of money
from foreign tourists. She has plenty of food."

Mrs Medina, who lived next door, heard Eldita.
"So you want your father to work hard all day
and then drive a taxi all night?" she said.
Elidta didn't dare say a word to Mrs Medina.

From downstairs came the sound of music.
Ta-tak, stomp stomp! Ta-tak, stomp stomp!
Eldita knew who was playing that guitar.
It was old Manuel coming to see them.

Eldita rushed to meet Manuel. "Abuelo! *"

Old Manuel could not see.

His eyes were as light as popcorn.

"What's the matter with our Eldie?" he said.

*Abeulo means Grandpa in Spanish.

Mrs Medina answered before Eldita did.
"She's upset because she didn't get
the main role in the ballet."

Old Manuel smiled and lifted his guitar.

"Even if my love blocks
her ears to my music,
even if the world doesn't
recognise my song,
it doesn't matter.

To me, precious is
my music and my song.
As long as music doesn't leave me,
I don't need anything else.
To me, precious is
my music and my song.
Eldie, my darling, Eldie,
what is precious to you?
Tell me, come and tell me."

12

Everyone looked at Eldita, and her mum said,
"What is the most important thing to you, Eldita?
Is it to be the main dancer in the ballet?"

Manuel smiled at the red-faced Eldita. He said, "Actually,
I'd give up my music for fried fish and a tomato."

They all laughed, trying to remember the last time
they had eaten a tomato. They were full of memories.

Old Manuel said tomato salads were best for fish dishes.
"It's like a song ready to explode in your mouth."

Granny Olla fell in love with a young man in a tomato patch.
"To this day, I remember the taste of fresh tomato."

Mrs Medina remembered the tomatoes her dad used to give her.
"Dad gave me the best ones before he went to sell them at the market."

When Eldita's mum was young, her mother made tomato soup.
"Eldita takes after me. She loves tomato soup, too."

It was true, but Eldita didn't want to talk about tomatoes.

Why talk about something you couldn't have?

It would only make her feel worse.

So Eldita went to the beach.

There were lots of people at the beach.
Eldita walked along the sand
and breathed in the sweet salt air.
She felt like a dancer on a stage.

Eldita danced, as light as a seagull.
Her feet flew over the sand as she twirled
and her arms fluttered in the air like wings.
As she bowed at the end of her performance,
she heard loud clapping and shouts of "Olé!"
A female tourist spoke in broken Spanish,
"You are a great dancer! That was wonderful!"

The woman said,
"Thank you for your lovely dance.
I would like to give you something.
I have a tomato I brought
from the hotel.
Do you like tomatoes?"

19

A tomato? Eldita couldn't believe her ears.
Mum, would be so surprised!

She stood for a long time,
holding the precious tomato.
So what if she didn't get
the main role in the ballet?
She loved to dance.
That was the most precious thing.

Holding the tomato in both hands,
Eldita ran home.
As she raced up the stairs,
she shouted, "Abuelo!"
But then
something terrible happened.

As she reached the landing,
she tripped and fell
on top of the tomato,
crushing it.
Too shocked for words,
she burst into tears.

Eldita's mother hugged her,
and Granny Olla said, "Too bad!"
Mrs Medina said, "The seeds burst out."
That was when Manuel played his guitar.

"Seeds are growing in Diego's garden.
Cover them with a blanket of dirt.
Let them drink the water down from heaven.
Ah-yi, ah-yi, ah-yi.
What will the seed become?
Will it be a block of gold?
A little bird? Or a little child?
Only the seed knows.
Not even Diego can tell.
But seeds are growing
in Diego's garden.
Ah-yi, ah-yi, ah-yi."

Grandma Olla smiled with pleasant surprise.
"I used to sing that song when I was a girl."

Eldita's mother said, "These tomato seeds will grow."

Mrs Medina said, "My father used to grow tomatoes.
You dry the seeds in the sun and then plant them in a pot.
Soon the seeds will have sprouts, then small plants.
You put the plants in soil in your garden
and they will grow and grow
and produce lots of tomatoes. Eldita's tomatoes!"

Eldita wiped her eyes and asked Mrs Medina,
"Even if our garden is full of rocks?"

"Of course!" said Mrs Medina,
"We'll work together to get rid of those rocks
so your plants have somewhere to grow."

Eldita and her mum put the seeds on a flat plate
and left them on the windowsill in the sun.
Manuel stroked his guitar and sang.
"Seeds like to hear songs," he said.

26

Eldita said to Manuel, "Abuelo, I've been thinking.
I like dancing. If I can dance, nothing else matters."

Old Manuel said, "Seeds also like dancing.
They are similar to me. They can't see but they can feel
a dance by the breeze it causes.
Why don't you dance for your seeds?"

One Sunday, everyone gathered in the garden
which was smooth and clean, with not a rock in sight.
One by one, Eldita planted the tomato seeds.
Old Manuel played his guitar and sang.

"Seeds are growing in Diego's garden.
Cover them with a blanket of dirt.
Let them drink the water down from heaven.
Ah-yi, ah-yi, ah-yi.

What will the seed become?
Will it be a block of gold?
A little bird? Or a little child?
No, no. The seeds know
and we do too.
These seeds growing in Eldita's garden
will become tomatoes.
Ah-yi, ah-yi, ah-yi."

29

The tomatoes grew well in Eldita's garden.
Now, more than ten years later,
not just tomatoes grow there, but other vegetables, too.

There are even some chickens that lay fresh eggs.
Soon other people started planting vegetables
in their gardens and on their balconies.
Neighbours came together to clear unused land
so they could grow their own food.

Today Eldita is a beautiful young woman
who still loves dancing.
Muy bien*, Eldita!

* Muy bien means well done in Spanish.

Urban Farming in Havana

Hello, boys and girls,

My name is Eldita and I'm from Havana, Cuba.
What do you know about my country?
It's very beautiful and I hope you will come to visit.
To be honest, Cuba isn't a wealthy country.
We don't have expensive clothes or houses
and most of our cars are old and rusty.
But we are rich in our love for one another.
My neighbours are kind and supportive.
We grow gardens in our courtyards
and share everything with each other.
We do not use chemical fertilisers
or anything else that might harm the earth.
When you come to visit, I will show you
how to grow organic crops.

Sincerely,
Eldita

Let's Think

Do we always have to farm large fields?

What is urban farming?

What does "organic produce" mean?

Have you grown food before?

CUBA: Eldita's Homeland

Atlantic Ocean

Bahamas

Gulf of Mexico

Cuba

Jamaica   Haiti

Belize

Honduras   Caribbean Sea

Nicaragua

Costa Rica

Area: 110,860 km²
Capital: Havana
Major Language: Spanish

The Republic of Cuba is an island country located in the Caribbean Sea, between the continents of South and North America. It consists of 1,600 islands. Cuba became a Spanish colony in the early 16th century and remained in Spanish possession until 1898. Cuba became an independent republic in 1959. Due to unfriendly relations with the United States of America, Cuba continues to face economic difficulties. Nevertheless, all education, from nursery to university, as well as medical services, is free.

Multi-ethnic Many people of different ethnicities and skin colours live in Cuba. The country is populated mostly by European descent and mulattos – people who are half African and half European. There are also African, Chinese and Indian ethnic groups. Although they are from different ethnic backgrounds, Cubans share a common interest in singing and telling stories.

The Economy of Cuba The sugar industry is the main source of income for the Cuban economy. Cuba also produces or trades coffee, cigars, prawns and minerals such as nickel.

Urban Farming in Cuba Cuba experienced difficult times in the 1990s, with the dissolution of the Soviet Union, and with the USA economic blockade. As supplies of imported goods such as oil, chemical fertilisers and other agricultural chemicals were cut off, the supply of food also diminished. One by one, people began to grow their own food in courtyards, gardens and on rooftops, Havana naturally developed urban farming.

Street festival in Havana, Cuba

What Is Urban Farming?

Urban farming is growing or producing food in a city or heavily populated area. People use available spaces - courtyards, rooftops, vacant blocks, city parks and playgrounds - to grow and produce food to be shared or sold. Urban farms are also called city farms or community gardens.

Urban Farming around the World

There are various forms of urban farming in major cities throughout the world, but urban farming in Cuba is considered an ideal model. This is because urban farms in Cuba provide much of the food

Produce grown in Havana being sold at a local market.

needed for the population. Approximately 80 per cent of the Cuban population lives in cities, which means that urban farming plays a significant role in overcoming food shortages. Today Cuba has become self-sufficient in the production of food.

In other modern cities, urban farming helps provide green spaces and gives people the opportunity to learn about growing food. However, the production of the food needed to feed the population still takes place on large farms.

Advantages of Urban Farming

1.   If food is grown close to the people who need it, then there is less energy and money needed to transport it from a faraway farm.

2.   Waste products like food scraps and rubbish are used to make compost to improve the soil.

3.   Using compost reduces the need for chemicals and fertilisers.

4.   Air quality in cities can improve as more plants grow there.

5.   Growing food is something fun everyone can do.

What Is an Organic Farm?

An organic farm does not use chemical fertilisers, growth hormones, herbicides, feed additives, antibiotics or any other artificial agricultural chemicals. Instead it uses only organic materials – like mineral waters, natural herbs, grass, food scraps, and other natural materials.

Food from an organic farm is called "organic produce" or "pesticide-free produce".

Urban farming relies on compost created with these organic materials instead of fertilisers.

Urban farming in Havana, Cuba

Urban farming in Chicago, USA

Let's Talk

1. Is there an urban farm or community garden near where you live?

2. Let's create an urban farm!
   Plant seeds in your garden.
   If you don't have a garden, plants seeds in a pot. For example, you could grow your own beans, lettuces, peppers, tomatoes, potatoes, eggplants and herbs.

3. If you can't grow your own vegetables, buy organic or pesticide-free produce whenever possible.

big & SMALL

Original Korean text by Yeo-rim Yun
Illustrations by Christopher Corr
Korean edition © Yeowon Media Co., Ltd.

This English edition published by Big & Small in 2015
by arrangement with Yeowon Media Co., Ltd.
English text edited by Joy Cowley
English edition © Big & Small 2015

ISBN: 978-1-925186-44-4

Printed in Korea